Mel Bay's
FLUTE METHOD

BY LOUIS HITTLER

Mel Bay's *Flute Method* is a new approach to teaching flute. This course contains a substantial amount of playing material in solo, exercise, scale, and duet forms. Range studies are included, along with studies designed to enhance fingering technique. As a supplement to this method, we recommend the following books:

Building Excellence® Series/Flute Solos
Building Excellence® Series/Technique Development for Beginning Flute
Building Excellence® Series/Tone Development for Beginning Flute
Flute Handbook
Solo Pieces for the Beginning Flutist

Copyright © 1978 and 1992 by Mel Bay Publications, Inc., Pacific, MO 63069.
All Rights Reserved. International Copyright Secured. Printed in U.S.A.

PARTS OF THE FLUTE

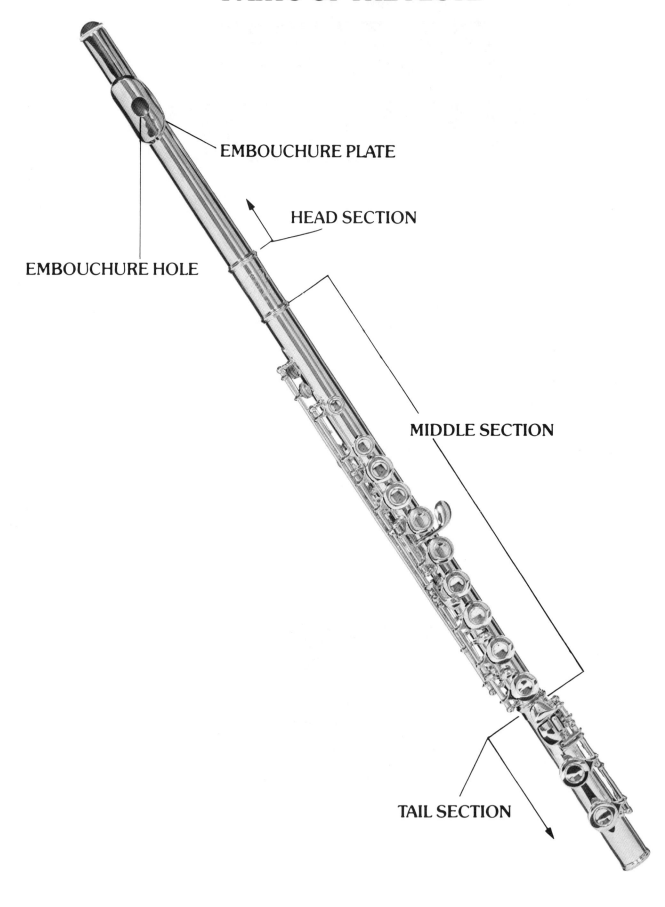

FLUTE FINGERING CHART

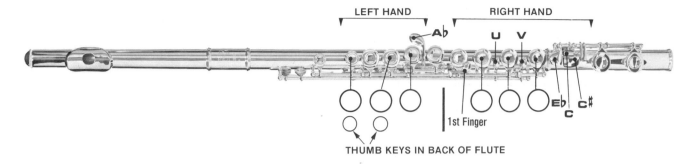

TO PLAY A "G" NOTE, FOR EXAMPLE...

- ● INDICATES FINGER PLATE CLOSED.
- ○ INDICATES FINGER PLATE OPEN.

LETTERS INDICATE KEY TO BE DEPRESSED.

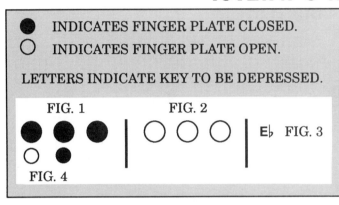

Fig. 1. The first three finger plates are closed by the first three fingers of the *left* hand.

Fig. 2. The next three finger plates remain open.

Fig. 3. The E♭ key is depressed with the little finger of the *right* hand.

Fig. 4. Thumb key is depressed with the left thumb.

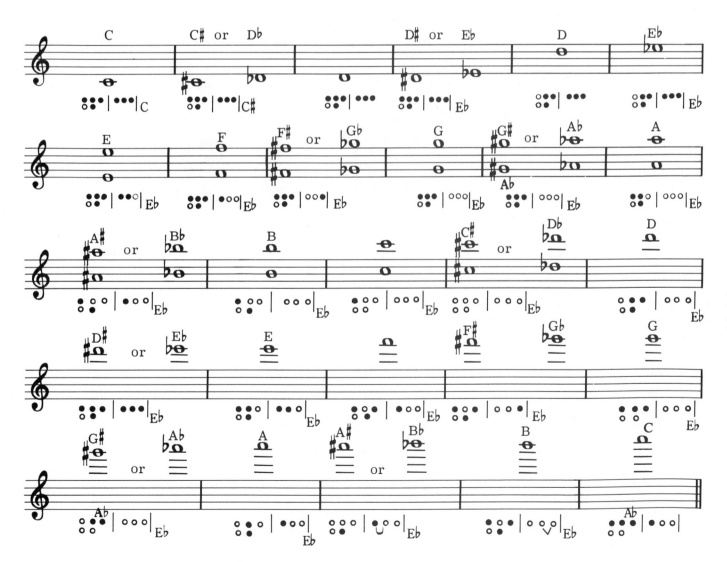

HOW TO ASSEMBLE AND TAKE CARE OF YOUR FLUTE

HOW TO TAKE CARE OF YOUR FLUTE

When assembling the flute, *Be Careful Not to Bend Any of The Keys.* Vaseline should be lightly spread on the joints so that they will easily engage. A light key oil should be placed on all working parts with a toothpick and a competent repair man should check the instrument at least once a year to make certain that all of the keys are properly aligned and that the pads are seating properly. A soft cloth placed on a swab rod should be used to wipe the inside of the instrument after each use. This will clean out any remaining moisture from the instrument when you put it back into your case. When putting the flute into the case always make certain:

(1) That the flute is placed in the case properly. Never force the case shut for this could seriously bend or damage keys.

(2) Make certain that the case is securely fastened so that when you carry the flute it does not fall open.

HOW TO ASSEMBLE YOUR FLUTE

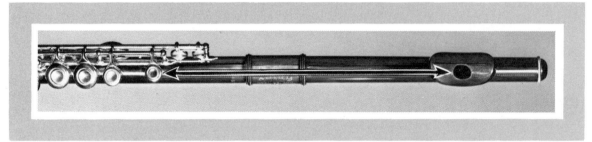

Fig. 5

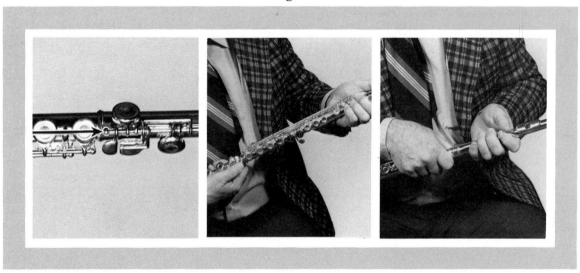

Fig. 6 *Fig. 7* *Fig. 8*

Put the flute together as indicated in Figures 5, 6, 7, and 8. The holes should be aligned as the arrows indicate in Figures 5 and 6.

FIGURE 7
First, we will connect the tail section with the middle section of the flute. The bottom or tail section of the flute should lie in the palm of your right hand. Pressure will be applied when assembling by the thumb of your right hand resting on the post. The palm of the left hand should nestle the back of the middle section of the flute. Do not put your fingers on the keys. This should not be necessary. You should be able to get a firm grip without grabbing the keys. Never force the instrument together. Apply gentle pressure so as not to damage any working parts. Finally, line up the keys as shown in Figure 5.

FIGURE 8
To insert the mouthpiece section into the flute, rest the middle section in the right hand. The mouthpiece section should rest in the left hand. The embouchure hole should line up with the keys as shown in Figure 6.

HOW TO HOLD THE FLUTE

To hold the instrument properly, rest the flute above the third joint of the first finger of the left hand (see picture). Keep the fingers slightly arched above the keys that they are to manipulate. The little finger of the right hand should be on the Eb key. The thumb of the right hand is kept on the underneath side of the flute between the first and second finger of the right hand. Remember, the flute must be parallel to the lips. Keep the elbows slightly away from the body and remember to keep your body relaxed.

FRONT VIEW   **SIDE VIEW**

PROPER SITTING POSITION

Observe the photograph showing proper sitting position when playing the flute. You will notice that the elbows are held out from the body in a loose manner so that your breathing may be free and easy. Do not slouch, sit in an upright position with the lower part of your back against the chair. Make certain that while you are sitting upright, you are not rigid.

GETTING A TONE ON THE FLUTE

EMBOUCHURE

The embouchure is the positioning of the lips for playing your instrument. In producing a tone on the flute, the proper embouchure is extremely important. First, it is important to keep the mouth muscles relaxed. Use the muscles at the corner of the mouth for gaining the proper tension. The center of the lip should remain relaxed. At first, close your lips naturally, blowing a stream of air thru a small opening in the center. *Do Not* tense the center of the upper and lower lip. After experimenting with your lip positioning, place the tone hole or embouchure hole on the lower lip so that approximately one-third of the hole is covered by the lower red portion of the lip. Now blow gently as described above. After producing a clear sound, place the tongue against the upper teeth, retracting the tongue as you blow. This will allow the air column to start. This is similiar to saying "tu." It is also called "tonguing."

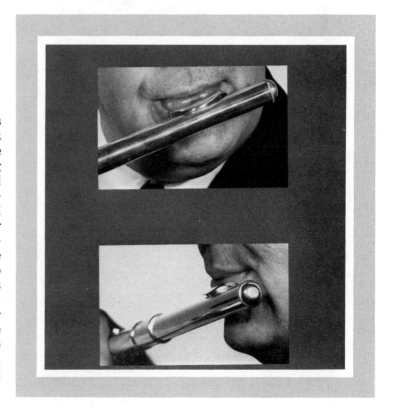

WHOLE NOTES, WHOLE RESTS, AND 4/4 OR (COMMON) TIME

4/4 time gets four beats to the bar. A whole note (𝅝) gets four counts (one and, two and, three and, four and). A whole rest (𝄻) gets four full counts, also (one and, two and, three and, four and).

OUR FIRST NOTES

"B" "A" "G" "C"

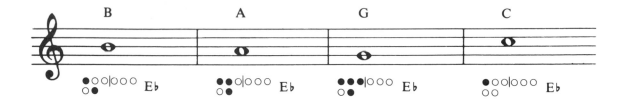

KEY OF "C"

NEW NOTE STUDIES

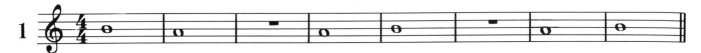
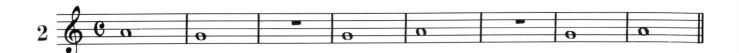

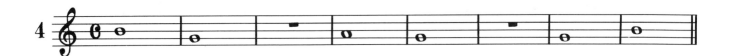

HALF NOTES

A half note looks like this: ♩. It receives two full counts (one and, two and). A half rest looks like this: ▬. It also receives two full counts. Notice that a whole rest hangs down from a line (▬), while a half rest sits on top of a line (▬).

Your air pressure begins when you start blowing the first note of the following study and continues until you reach the rest. Breathe deeply on the rest. Remember to tongue each note.

NEW NOTES

"F" "E" "D"

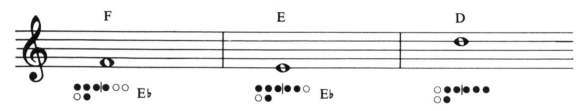

NEW NOTE STUDIES

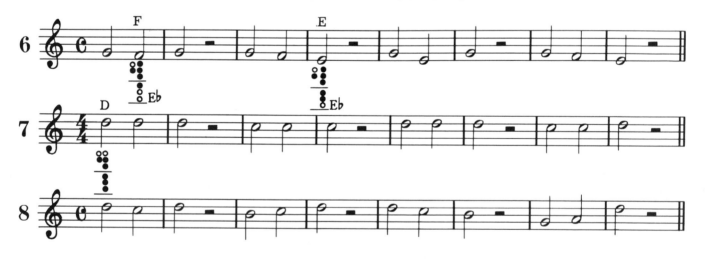

COUNTING SONG #1

QUARTER NOTES

A quarter note looks like this: 𝅗𝅥 or ♩. It receives one full count (one and). A quarter rest looks like this: 𝄽. It also receives one full count.

QUARTER NOTE SONGS

"E"   "F"   "G"

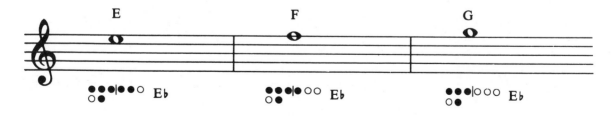

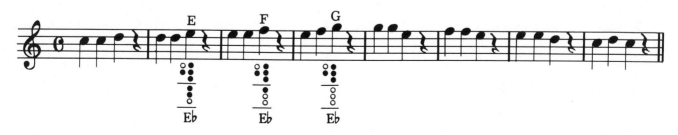

THE TIE

A tie looks like this: ⌒ . When a tie appears, tongue the first note and hold (do not tongue) the second note that it is tied to.

𝄻 = *Breath mark. Where this sign appears, take a breath.*

Remember: High notes will require more blowing effort at first.

TIE SONG

ARRANGED BY BILL BAY

DOTTED HALF NOTE

A dot after a note gives the note half of the time value of the preceding note. A dotted half note looks like this: 𝅗𝅥. It gets three full counts (one and, two and, three and).

SKIPPING

COUNTING SONG #2

3/4 TIME

In 3/4 time we have three beats per measure, and a quarter note receives one full beat. Count "one and, two and, three and," etc.

"A"   "B"   "C"

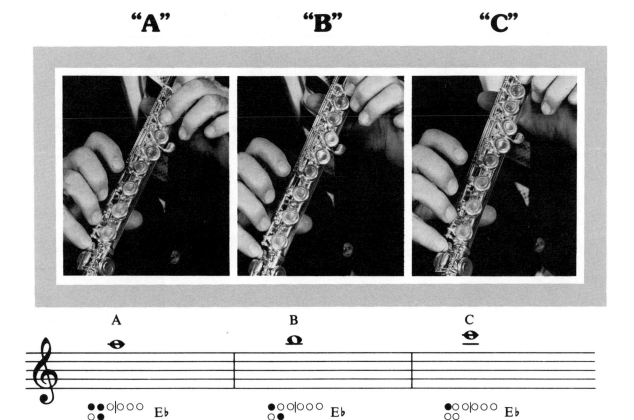

NEW NOTE STUDY

2/4 TIME

In 2/4 time we have two beats for each measure (one and, two and). Each quarter note gets a full beat.

COUNTING SONG #3

"B♭"   "F#"

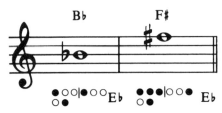

USE OF SHARPS AND FLATS

A flat looks like this: ♭. It lowers a note by a half tone or step.

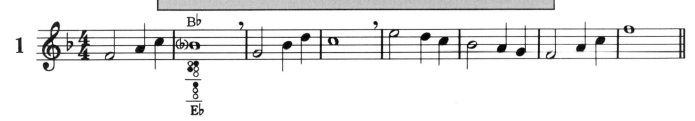

KEY OF "F"

One flat in the key signature of a song means that we are in the key of "F." In the key of "F" all "B"s are played as "B♭"s unless otherwise indicated.

"F" SCALE

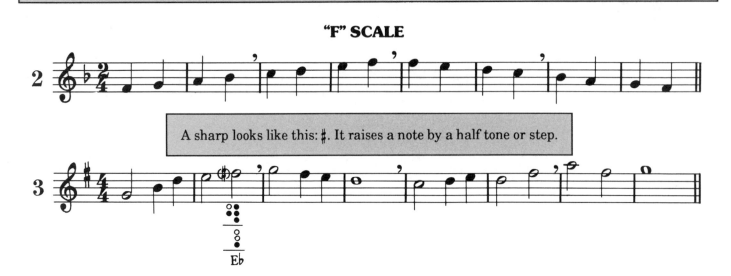

A sharp looks like this: ♯. It raises a note by a half tone or step.

KEY OF "G"

One sharp in the key signature of a song means that we are in the key of "G." In the key of "G" all "F"s are played as "F#"s unless otherwise indicated.

"G" SCALE

A natural sign looks like this: ♮. It cancels a sharp or flat.

A SONG OF FLATS AND SHARPS

RED RIVER VALLEY

LONDON BRIDGE

THE SLUR

A slur is a large bracket that connects one or more notes. When a slur occurs, tongue only the first note and merely finger all other notes under the slur.

REPEAT

A repeat sign looks like this: ||: or :||. When the sign :|| occurs, go back to this sign: ||: and repeat, or go back to the beginning if no other repeat sign is written.

In the following song:
1. Play A to B.
2. Repeat A to B and then go on to the end.

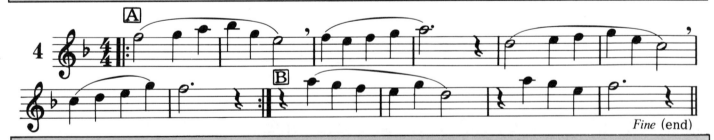

In the following song:
1. Play A through the first ending and repeat back to A.
2. On the second time through, take the second ending instead of the first ending and go on to the end.

ALLE BREVE (𝄵)

"Alle Breve" means "cut time." The symbol is 𝄵. It means that we have two beats per measure and each half note gets one beat. All notes therefore get half the value they received in 4/4 time.

Time values in Alle Breve:
A whole note gets two counts. A whole rest gets two counts.
A half note gets one count. A half rest gets one count.
A quarter note gets a half count. A quarter rest gets a half count.

COUNTING SONG #4

SOLOS

CAMPTOWN RACES

WHEN THE SAINTS COME MARCHING IN

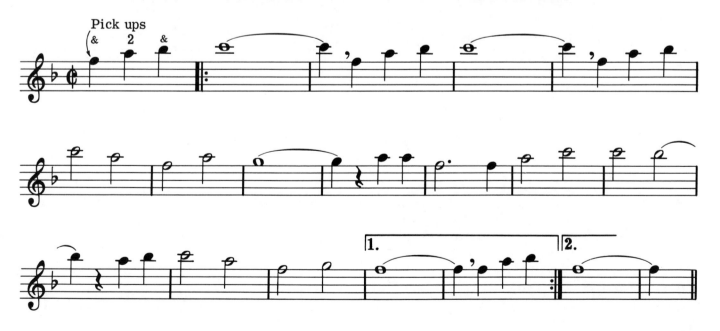

EIGHTH NOTE REST (GETS 1/2 COUNT)

Breathe During Rest

COUNTING SONG #5

THE TRIPLET

A triplet is a group of three notes played in the time of two notes of the same kind.

DOTTED QUARTER AND EIGHTH NOTES

D.S. AL FINE

When you see the phrase "D.S. al Fine," go back to this sign: 𝄋 and play until you reach the word "Fine," which means "The End." Do not play any repeats on a "D.S. al Fine."

HYMN

MARCH MILITAIRE

BY BILL BAY

AMAZING GRACE

ARRANGED BY BILL BAY

20

NEW NOTES

"E♭"   "D"   "C#"   "C#"

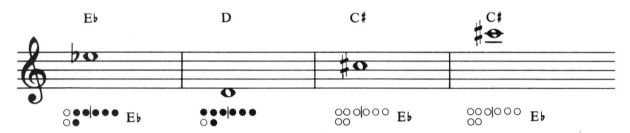

KEY OF "B♭"

In the key of "B♭" we have two flats, "B♭" and "E♭."

"B♭" SCALE

KEY OF "D"

In the key of "D" we have two sharps, "F♯" and "C♯."

"D" SCALE

HIGH NOTES

The high notes, or notes above the staff, are fingered differently than those we've previously learned. The fingerings are new and slightly difficult, so they should be practiced slowly and patiently at first. Gradually, you will develop more finger dexterity. The exercises below and the following lesson should be practiced until perfect and playable with ease before proceeding to the next lessons.

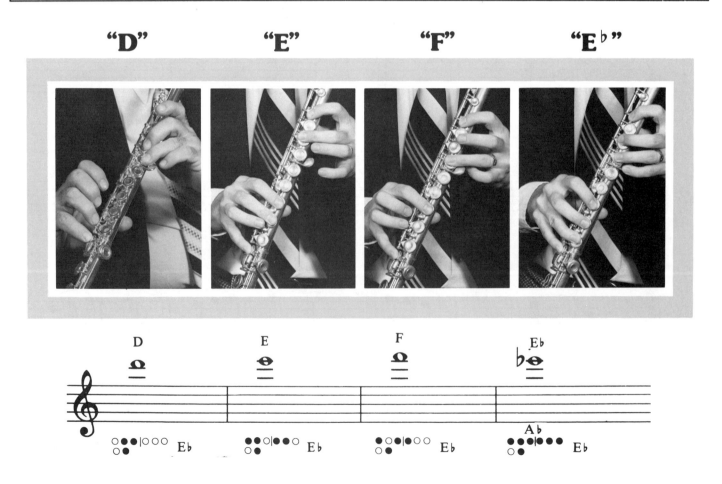

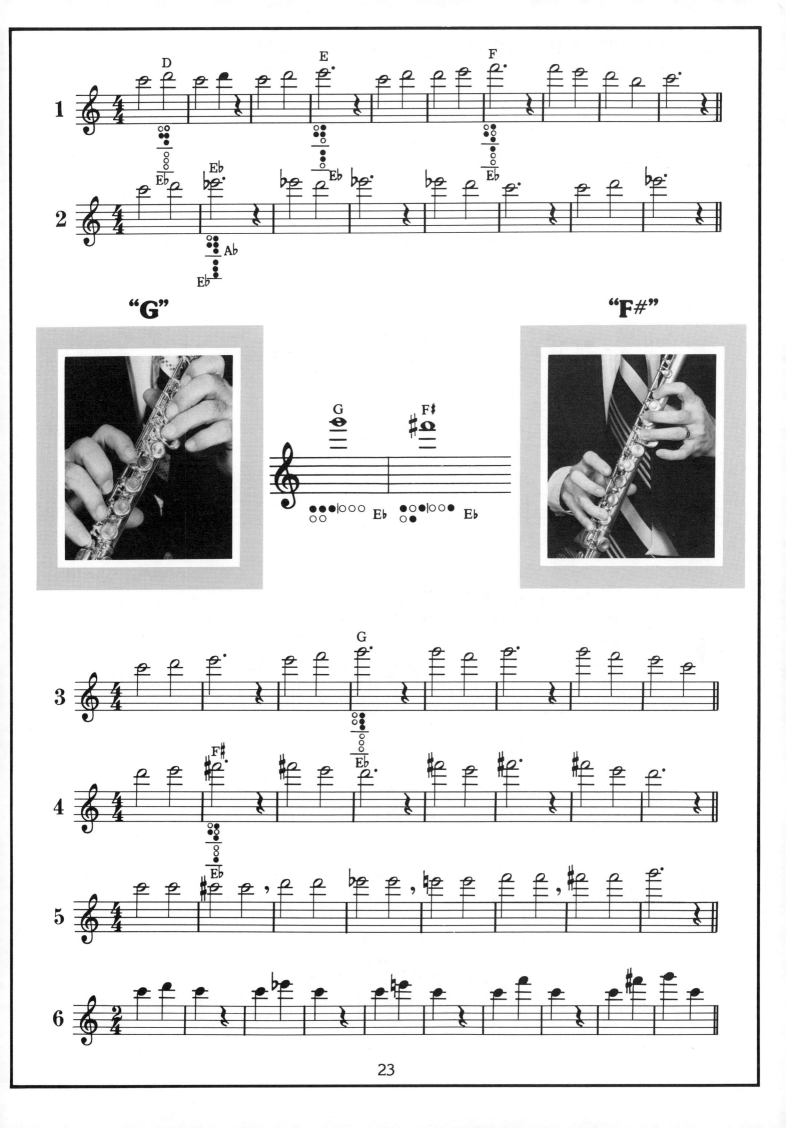

THIRD REGISTER NOTES (FINGER EXERCISES)

"C" SCALE

"Bb" SCALE

"D" SCALE

"G" SCALE

DUETS
PRAISE TO THE LORD

ARRANGED BY BILL BAY
Joachim Neander 1680

TALLIS CANNON

ARRANGED BY BILL BAY
Thomas Tallis 1567

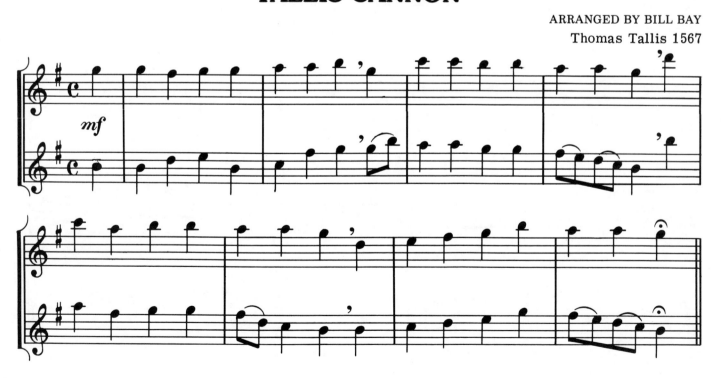

HOME ON THE RANGE

This means go back to sign (𝄋) and play to fine or Finish
D.S. al Fine

JEANIE WITH THE LIGHT BROWN HAIR

16th NOTES

A sixteenth note looks like this: ♪. Several sixteenth notes together look like this: ♫ or ♬. A sixteenth rest looks like this: 𝄿. It takes two sixteenth notes to equal one eighth note, and four sixteenth notes to equal one quarter note.

TABLE OF NOTES AND RESTS

OTHER SIXTEENTH NOTE STUDIES AND SIXTEENTH RESTS (𝄿)

SIXTEENTH NOTE SONG

SIMILARITY BETWEEN SIXTEENTH NOTES AND EIGHTHS PLAYED IN CUT TIME

COUNTING SONG #6

COVENTRY CAROL

ARRANGED BY BILL BAY
Old English Carol

SARABANDE

ARRANGED BY BILL BAY
Handel

O FOR A THOUSAND TONGUES TO SING

ARRANGED BY BILL BAY

DOTTED EIGHTHS AND SIXTEENTHS

A dotted eighth note followed by a sixteenth note is a common figure in music. Practice the following study until the timing is felt and understood.

DOTTED EIGHTHS & SIXTEENTHS
THE SIMILARITY TO DOTTED QUARTER AND 8TH IN CUT TIME.

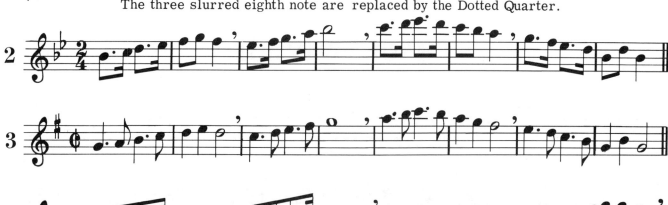

COUNTING SONG #7

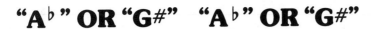

KEY OF "E♭"

In the key of "E♭" we have 3 flats, "B♭," "E♭," and "A♭."

"E♭" SCALE

TRIPLETS AGAIN

A SONG OF TWO KEYS

6/8 AND 3/8 TIME

So far we have studied 4/4, 2/4, and 3/4 time, where the quarter note gets one count or two eighth notes get one count. In 6/8 and 3/8 time, an eighth note gets one count.

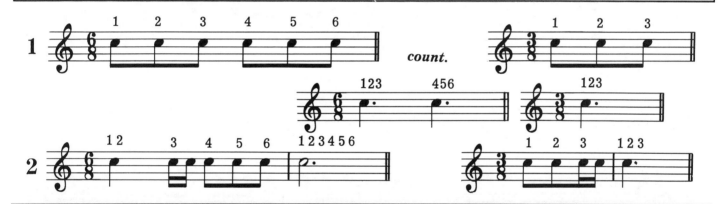

As in cut time, where we play two quarter notes in one beat, in 6/8 time we also count two beats in a bar; but here we play three eighth notes or their equivalent in one count and treat the three eighth notes similar to eighth-note triplets — playing three of them evenly in one beat.

Play slowly at first in 6/8, then count two beats to the bar, treating the eighth notes as triplets.

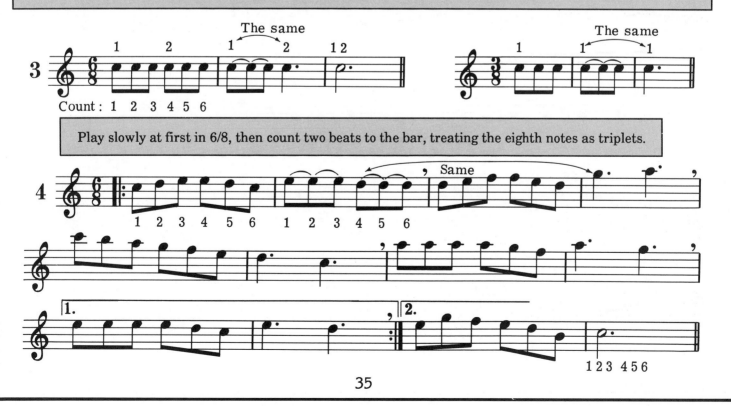

PLAY WITH SIX BEATS TO THE BAR — THEN WITH TWO BEATS

COUNTING SONG #8

DRINK TO ME ONLY WITH THINE EYES

BELIEVE ME, IF ALL
THOSE ENDEARING YOUNG CHARMS

STACCATO

"Staccato" means to play the notes short. A dot above a note signifies "staccato" or "short." To play staccato, give the note half the value indicated:

STACCATO SONG

DYNAMIC MARKINGS

	pp	*p*	*mp*	*mf*	*f*	*ff*
Italian	Pianissimo	Piano	Mezzo piano	Mezzo forte	Forte	Fortissima
English	Very soft	Soft	Medium soft	Medium loud; normal playing volume	Bold, strong	Very loud, but controlled; never blaring

Crescendo

Start soft and gradually increase the air until a volume of *f* (forte) is reached.

Decrescendo

Gradually decrease air flow until volume of *p* (piano) is reached.

Crescendos and decrescendos are accomplished by gradually increasing or decreasing the air flow. Be certain that the tone does not waver in the process. The position of the tongue and lips should remain constant, and there should be no variance in the pitch or quality of the tone.

39

LIP EXERCISES

simile Means to use the same dynamics till other wise indicated.

MENUET

ARRANGED BY BILL BAY
Nichelmann

MINOR MELODY

Bill Bay

KEY OF "A♭"

In the key of "A♭" we have four flats, "B♭," "E♭," "A♭," and "D♭."

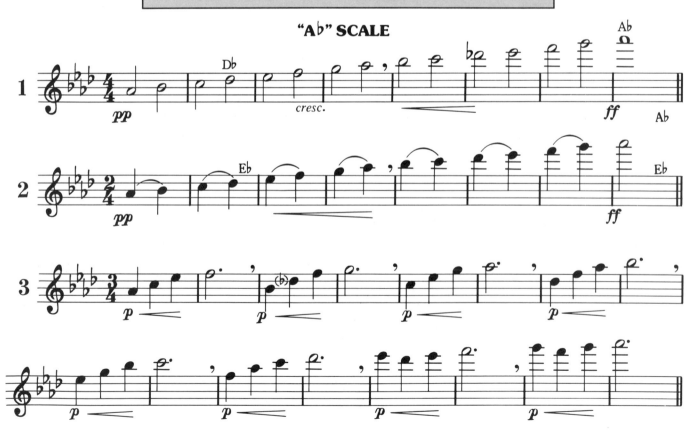

"A♭"-"E" CONTINUED

Note: "D♯" is fingered like "E♭."

MENUETT

ARRANGED BY BILL BAY
J.S. Bach

I SAW THREE SHIPS

ARRANGED BY BILL BAY
Old English

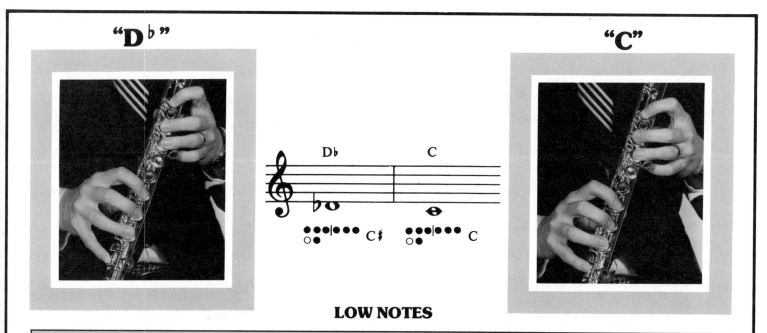

SCALE STUDIES

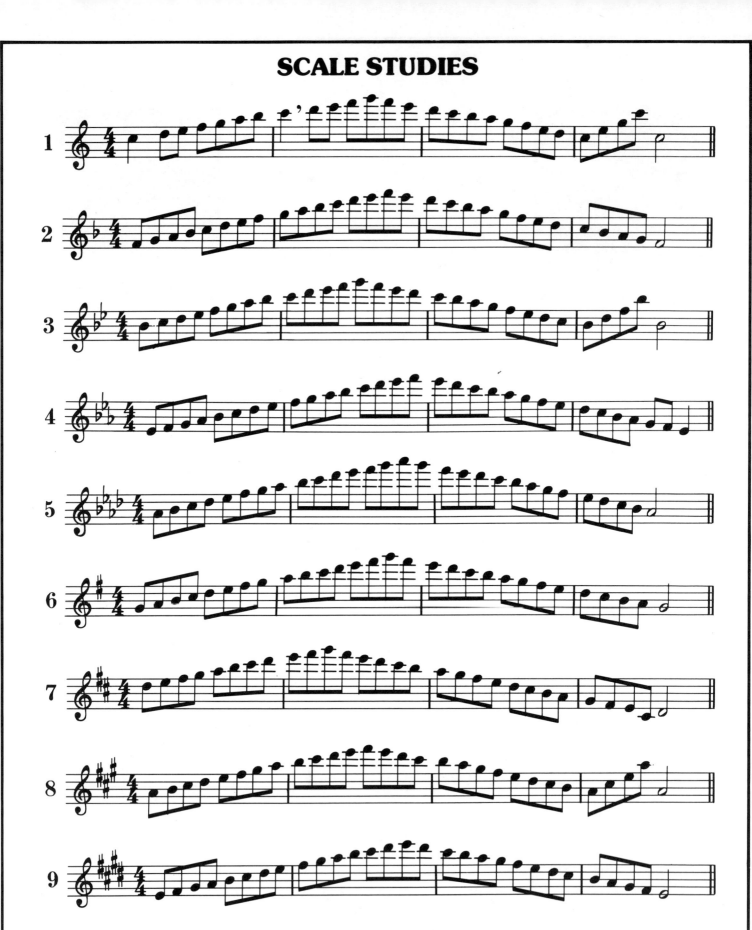

CHROMATIC SCALE

SOLOS FOR TONE

CRADLE SONG

Brahms

CHANSON TRISTE

Tschaikovsky

6/8 AND 3/8 SONGS
IRISH WASHER WOMAN

BOUNCING ALONG

SIXTEENTH NOTE SOLOS
NORWEGIAN DANCE
Grieg

CARCASSI'S SONG

TONAL STUDIES

Good tone quality is essential. The following studies will aid in improving tone. Practice them slowly at first (metronome speed of 72). Listen to your tone while playing to be certain that it sounds full. Practice at "forte" at first, then follow the dynamic markings.

⌒ = *a pause or fermata*

When this symbol appears, hold the note longer than its usual time value.

// = *caesura or cut*

When this symbol appears, come to an abrupt or sudden stop. Make a definite break before starting the next note.

ETUDE BY SOR

ARRANGED BY BILL BAY

MINOR MELODY

Bill Bay

IRISH MELODY

ARRANGED BY BILL BAY

FACILITY EXERCISES

FACILITY CONTINUED

FACILITY CONTINUED

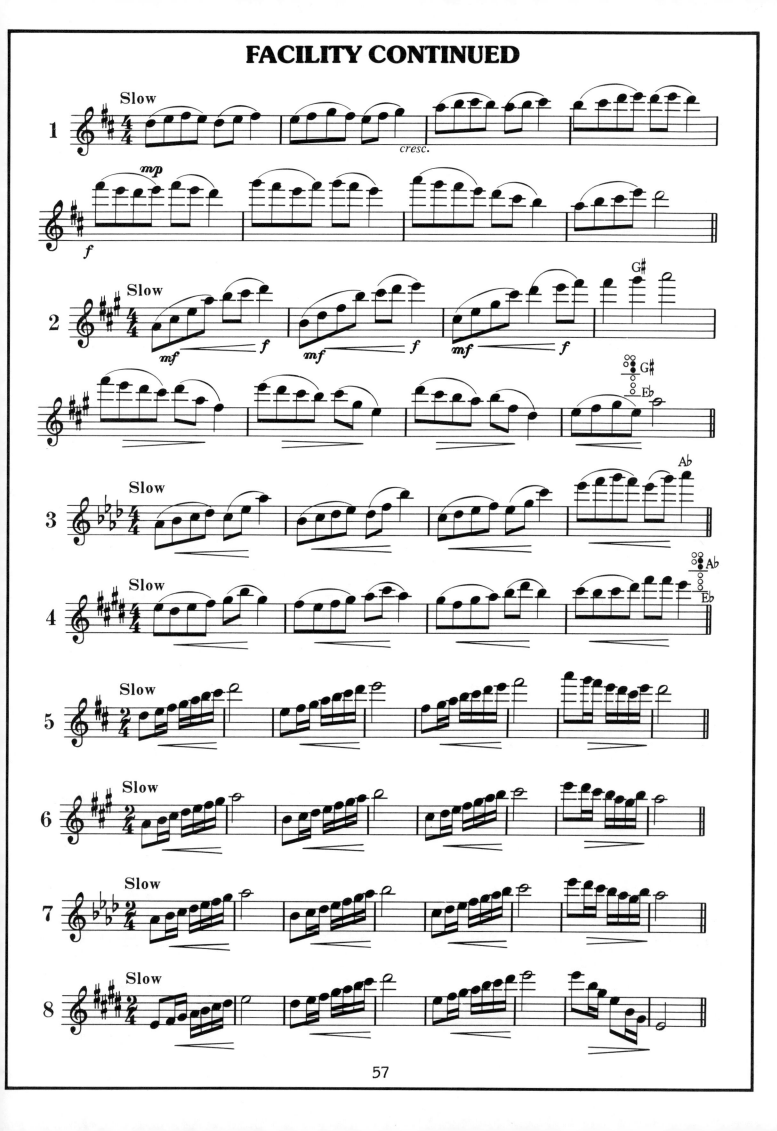

POLKA DUET

ANGELS WE HAVE HEARD ON HIGH

ARRANGED BY BILL BAY
French Carol

SONATINA

After the vibrato studies on the last pages of this book have been practiced, the student should return to this page and apply the vibrato techniques.

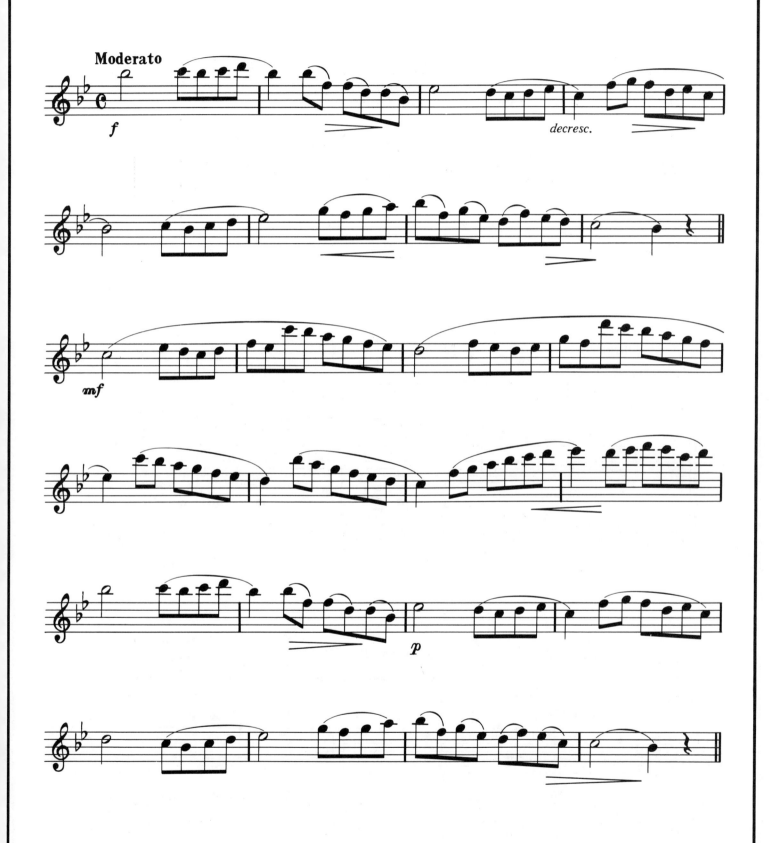

SYNCOPATION

"Syncopation" means to accent certain beats which ordinarily would not receive such an accent. It is used in all forms of music and is exceptionally prevalent in pop music. Once the basic note patterns commonly found in syncopation are learned and recognized, it is easy. Syncopated notes are usually played in an accented style. In the following studies, practice line A first, then line B (tie added). Finally, line C has the same time value as line B.

SYNCOPATION CONTINUED

CUT TIME

SYNCOPATION FOR TWO

MORE SYNCOPATION SONGS

BILL BAILEY

ARRANGED BY BILL BAY

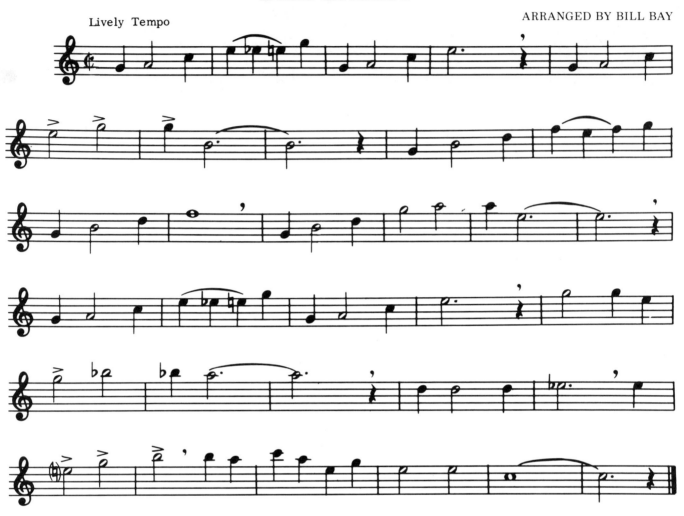

THE ENTERTAINER

ARRANGED BY BILL BAY

JOPLIN

FACILITY IN MORE DIFFICULT KEYS

EASTER HYMN
STUDY IN THE KEY OF "D♭"

ARRANGED BY BILL BAY

NOW THANK WE ALL OUR LORD
STUDY IN THE KEY OF "E"

ARRANGED BY BILL BAY
Johann Crüger

NOW THE DAY IS OVER
STUDY IN THE KEY OF "B"

ARRANGED BY BILL BAY

STACCATO DUET

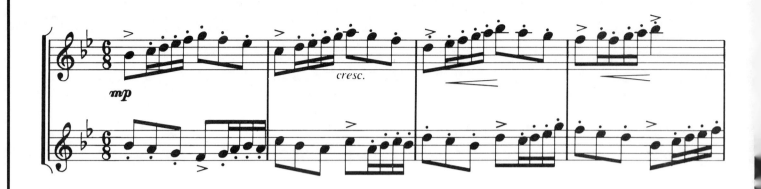
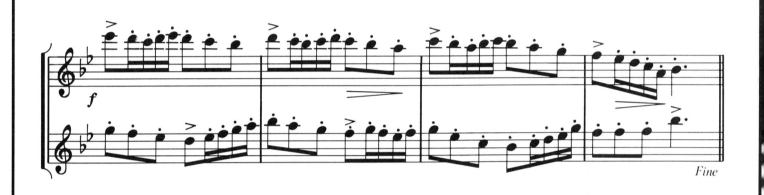
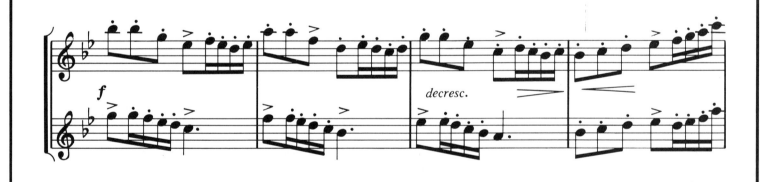
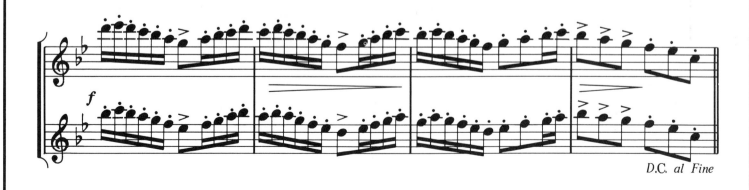

FURTHER HIGH NOTE STUDIES

In music, one frequently has to play notes one octave higher than written. This is indicated by the sign *"8va."* When this appears, play the notes one octave higher and be sure to **use proper high-note fingerings.** Practice the following studies slowly.

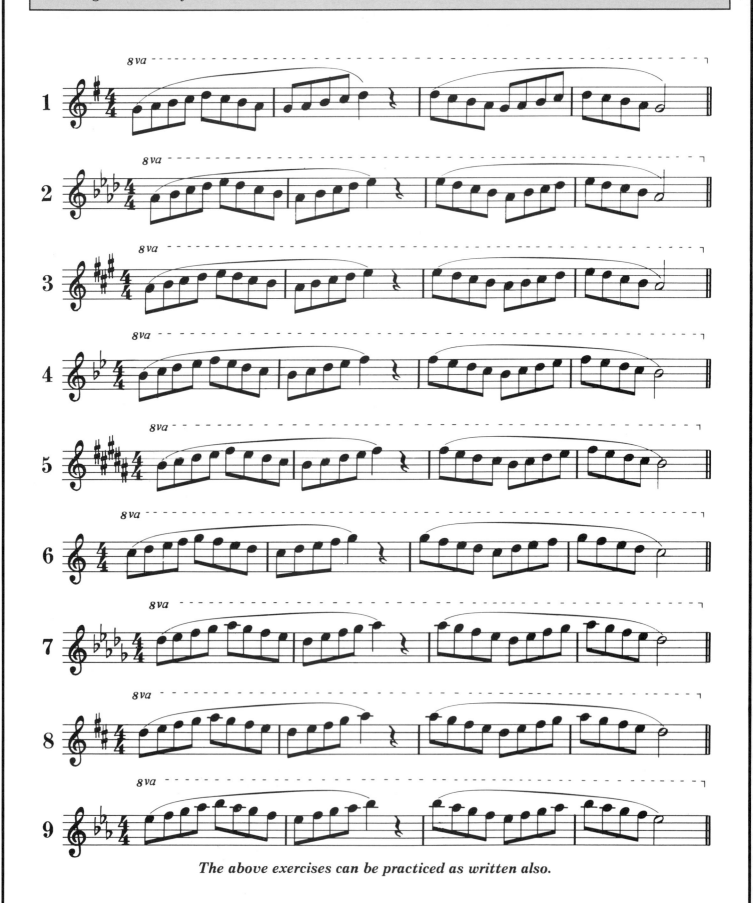

The above exercises can be practiced as written also.

HIGH NOTE DUET

SCOTTISH DUET

SCENES THAT ARE BRIGHTEST

After the vibrato studies on the last pages of this book have been practiced, the student should return to this page and apply the vibrato techniques.

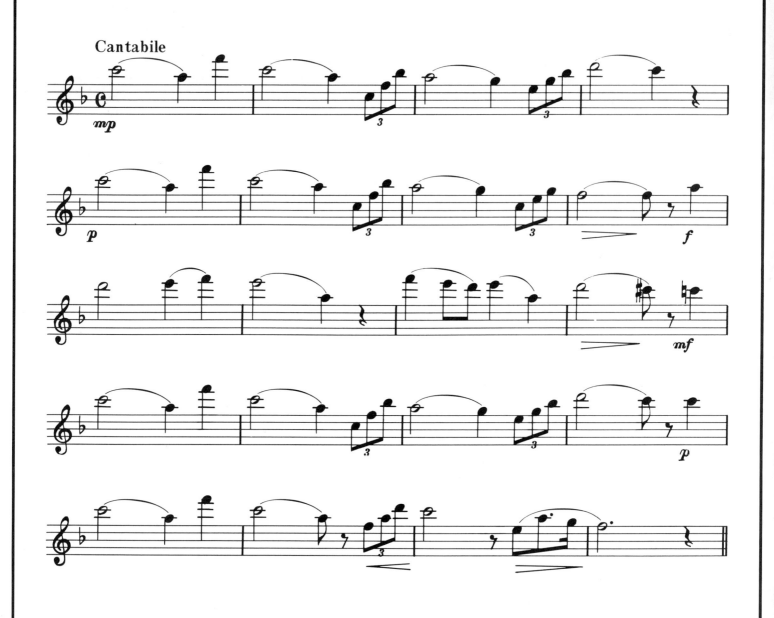

ORIGINAL MELODY

CHROMATIC STUDIES

CHROMATIC DUETS

DAILY STUDIES IN THIRDS

"G" HARMONIC MINOR (RELATED TO "B♭" MAJOR)

"D" MAJOR

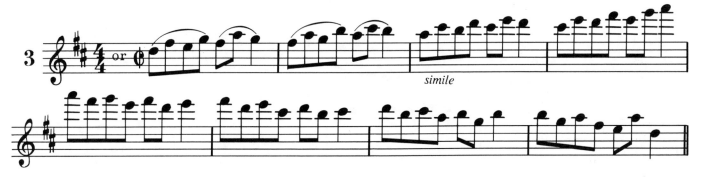

"B" HARMONIC MINOR (RELATED TO "D" MAJOR)

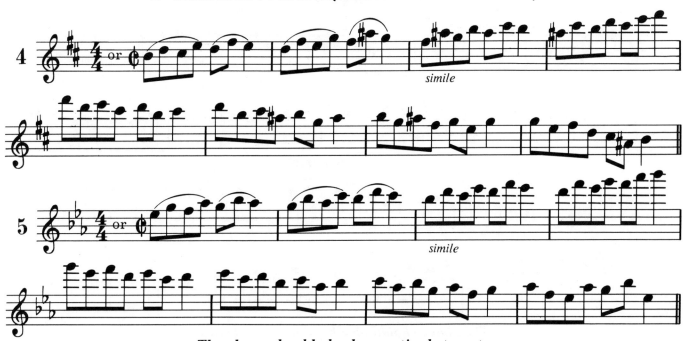

The above should also be practiced staccato

DAILY THIRDS CONTINUED

"A♭" MAJOR

"F" MINOR (HARMONIC)

"A" MAJOR

"F#" MINOR

"D♭" MAJOR

The above should also be practiced staccato

MINUET

ARRANGED BY BILL BAY
Mozart

FRENCH SONG

ARRANGED BY BILL BAY
Tschaikowsky

DAILY SCALES AND ARPEGGIOS

DAILY SCALES AND ARPEGGIOS

FAREWELL

ARRANGED BY BILL BAY
Purcell

PASSEPIED

ARRANGED BY BILL BAY
Telemann

GRACE NOTES

Grace notes are notes used to enhance music. They have no time value, but borrow their value from either the note they precede or the note that they follow. The period and style of the compositions we are playing determine how we will play the grace notes. In older music, grace notes receive their value from the note they precede. In some newer music, the grace notes receive their value from the note they follow. Study the following example:

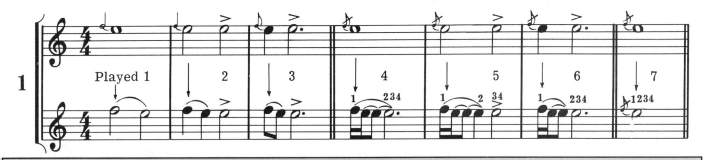

The grace notes in the first three bars are long grace notes and are seldom used. Grace notes in the last three bars are sometimes played before the beat (as in the last bar).

The grace notes in the following studies should be practiced ahead of the beat and on the beat.

The following grace notes are usually played before the beat.

LE TAMBOURIN

ARRANGED BY BILL BAY
Jean-Philippe Rameau

SERENADE

After the vibrato studies on the last pages of this book have been practiced, the student should return to this page and apply the vibrato techniques.

ritard. (Slow Down)

CHORD ETUDE

SCALE ETUDE

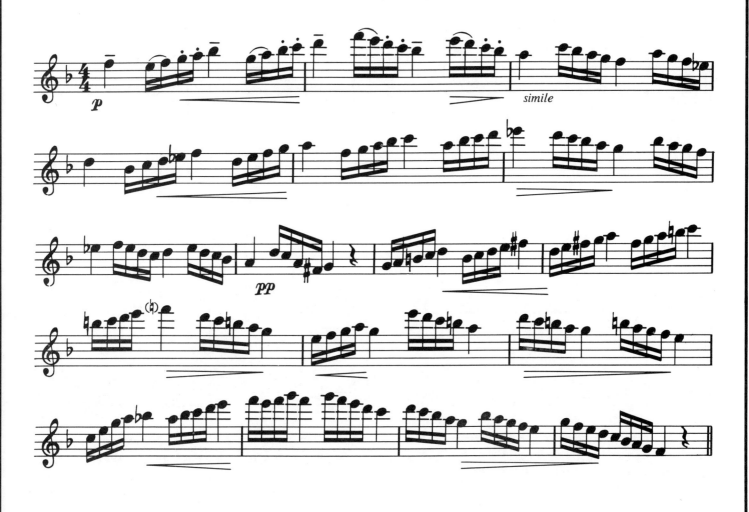

SIXTEENTH NOTE TRIPLETS

In the above duet, do not take the first ending on Da Capo ("D.C."). It might also be advisable to keep the left thumb on key W throughout (except where "B♮" occurs).

DIFFICULT SLURS

Practice these exercises slowly at first for relaxed lip movement. Listen carefully to intonation in the octave skips.

87

ARTICULATION ETUDES

MORE ARTICULATION

SONGS USING STACCATO

CARMEN

Allegro (Means lively, fast)

Bizet

PAGANINI

Allegro

TWO NEW HIGH NOTES

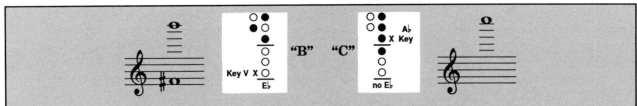

These two new high notes, high "B" and "C," are a little difficult but should be learned at this point.

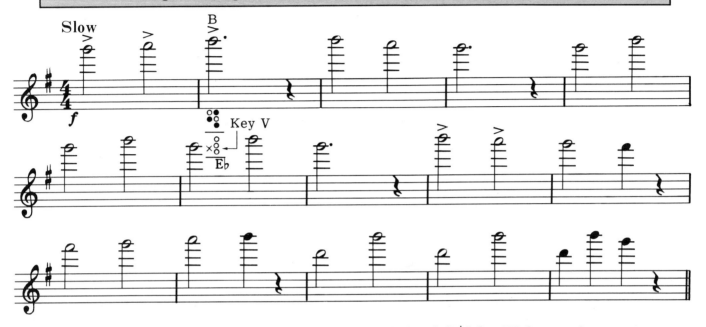

High "B" and high "F#" cannot be played with thumb "B♭" (key W) depressed.

This page should be practiced very slowly in order to become acquainted with the intricate fingering of high "C" and "B."

VIBRATO

The use of vibrato is a controversial subject. It should always be used in good taste to enhance the music played. Vibrato can be produced in several ways (diaphragm or throat). If these instructions are followed carefully, it will be produced properly. Vibrato use and speeds must at all times be controlled by the performer so that a perfect match with other players can be attained.

In Exercise 1, play a metronome speed of 68, using the tongue to attack notes and taking a deep breath on eighth rests. After it can be played smoothly and evenly, play it again using a breath attack (stopping and starting the breath). It should feel like you are blowing against your lips. Gradually blend the stopping and starting of the breath into an even vibrato.

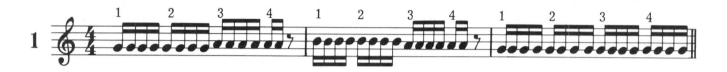

At this point you will notice that you are putting four vibratos on each count. Practice the following exercise at different speeds (metronome speeds 62–68–72–78).

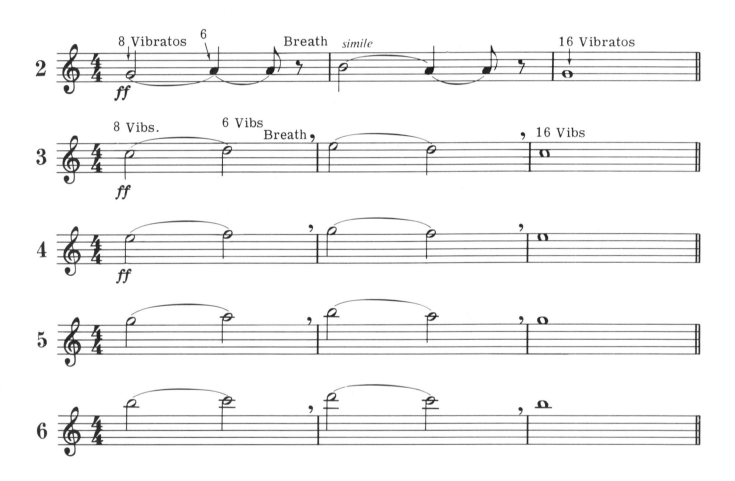

Repeat the above exercises using three vibratos per beat (metronome tempo 82–86–92). Get this under control, then practice slowly at metronome tempo 60 using six vibratos per beat. After vibrato control is learned in this way, the performer should not count vibratos per beat but use an even, controlled vibrato according to the style and interpretation of the music.

VIBRATO

In the following short songs, I will indicate how many vibratos to use on each note at certain metronome tempos. These should be brought under control. Keep your vibrato very even, watching for diminuendos to prepare for breathing (metronome tempo 68–72).

The above exercises should now be practiced at metronome speed 54–60 with six vibratos. Then at 86–92–100 with three vibratos per beat. Again, **do not** rely on counting vibratos per beat! This is done just to gain control. At the beginning of this book, the daily tonal studies should now be practiced with vibrato.

The following should be played with a straight tone on the notes where there is no curved line and a controlled vibrato on the notes under the curved line.

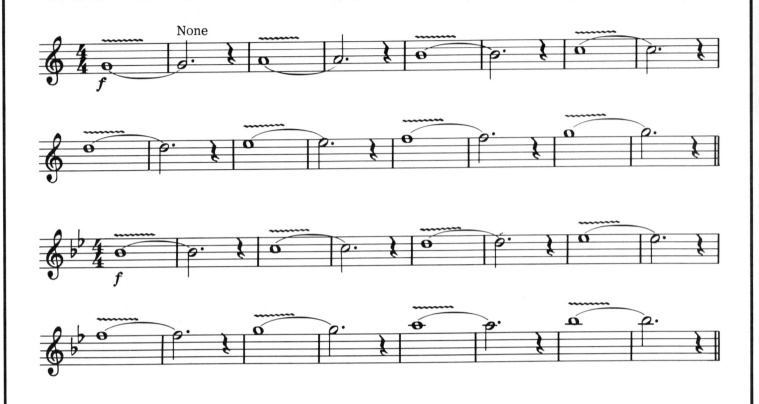

HOME SWEET HOME

The above exercises should be played in cut time — **no** vibrato on quarter notes, and four vibratos per beat on half and whole notes. Play at different tempos and do not count vibratos, but use a controlled, even vibrato.

MELODY WITH VIBRATO

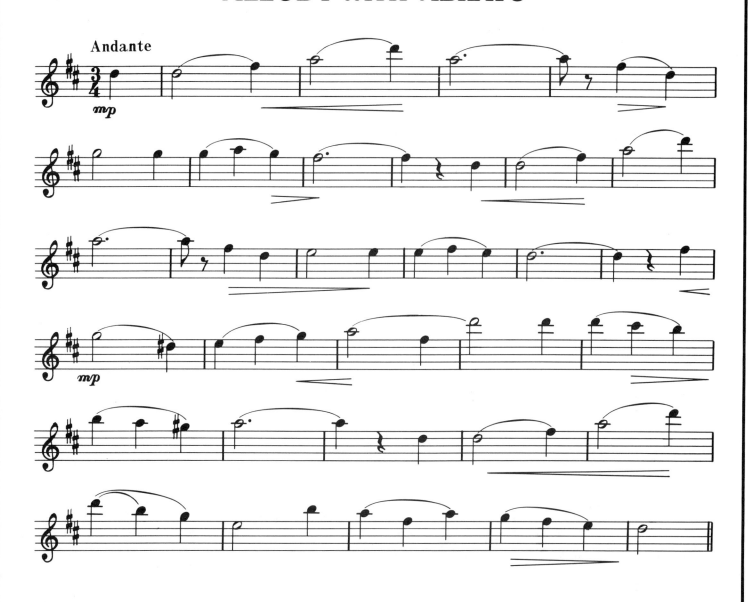

VIBRATO ON HALF NOTE SONG

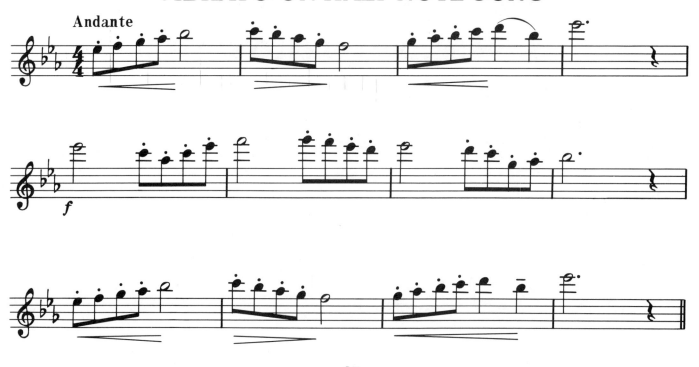

RONDO

TONGUE AND VIBRATO SONG

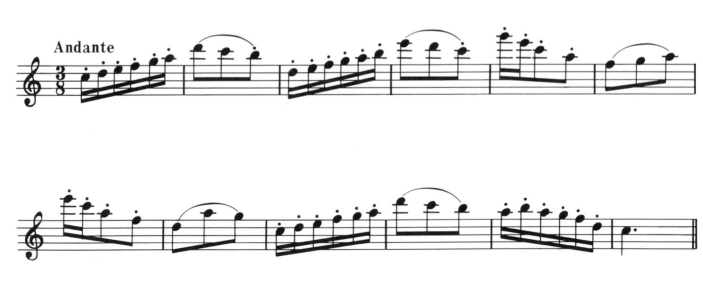

GYPSY RONDO (TECHNICAL SOLO)

NEW TIME SIGNATURES

3 = 3 beats per measure
2 = each half note gets 1 full beat

In 3/2 time: 𝅝 = 2 beats   𝅗𝅥. = 1½ beats   𝅗𝅥 = 1 beat   ♩ = ½ beat   ♪ = ¼ beat

HYMN

ARRANGED BY BILL BAY

German melody 1623

6 = 6 beats per measure
4 = each quarter note receives 1 full beat

MEDITATION

Bill Bay

THE WILD HORSEMEN

ARRANGED BY BILL BAY
Robert Schumann

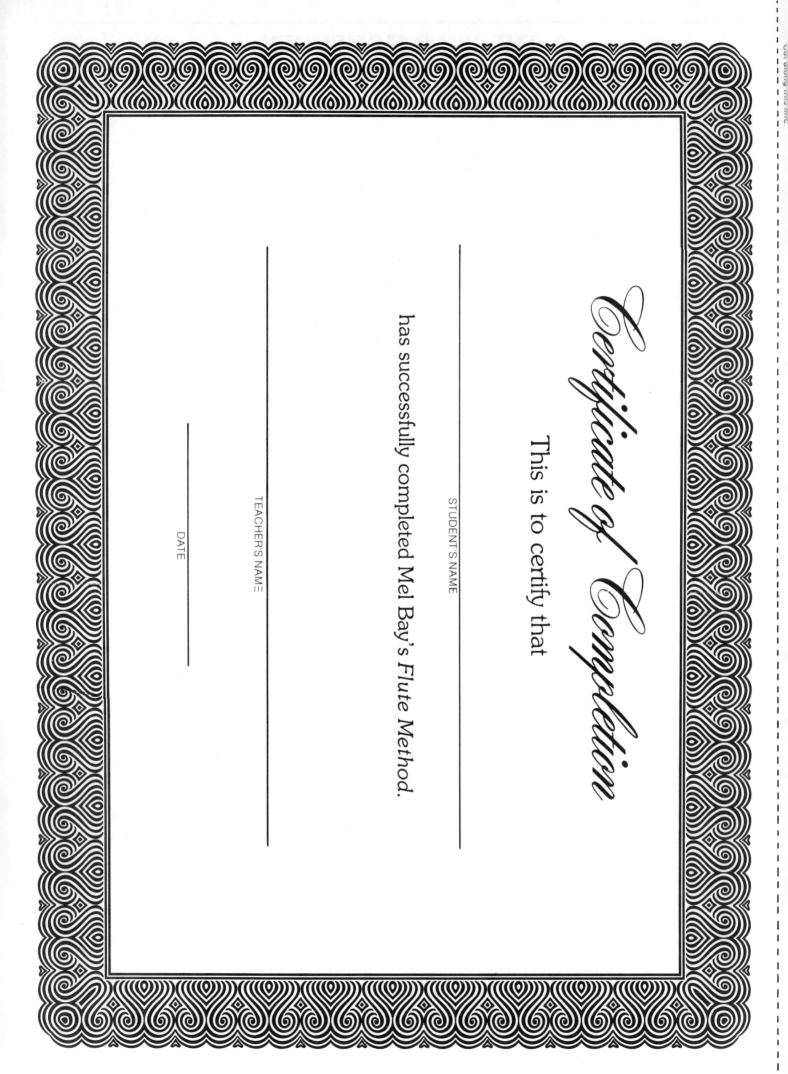